This book belongs to:

. . . .

To my lovely Mum. A.S.

To Mum, Dad, Chris, and Terry with love from the very privileged baby of the family! L.M.

OXFORD
UNIVERSITY PRESS

Great Clarendon Street, Oxford OX2 6DP
Oxford University Press is a department of the University of Oxford.
It furthers the University's objective of excellence in research, scholarship,
and education by publishing worldwide. Oxford is a registered trade mark of
Oxford University Press in the UK and in certain other countries

Text copyright © Amber Stewart 2009
Illustrations copyright © Layn Marlow 2009

The moral rights of the author and illustrator have been asserted
Database right Oxford University Press (maker)

First published as *Just Like Tonight* in 2009
This edition first published in 2018

British Library Cataloguing in Publication Data
Data available

ISBN: 978-0-19-276855-1

10 9 8 7 6 5 4 3 2 1

Printed in China

Paper used in the production of this book is a natural,
recyclable product made from wood grown in sustainable forests.
The manufacturing process conforms to the environmental
regulations of the country of origin.

My First Milestones

Goodnight, Sleep Tight

Amber Stewart · Layn Marlow

OXFORD
UNIVERSITY PRESS

It was bedtime for Button.

'My little bear cub must be tired,' said Mummy,
'after such a busy day.'
'Sweet dreams,' said Daddy.

As they kissed him goodnight,
Button thought sleepily about his day
and wondered what his dreams might bring.

He remembered lazing in the
early morning sunshine . . .

climbing with his
big sisters . . .

playing by their
favourite pool . . .

and finding
interesting insects,

even a ladybird with three spots on one wing and not
a single spot on the other. Button found it on the fallen
tree that looked like a big bear asleep in the grass.

Button had forgotten about the
big, scary tree-bear until that very moment.
Supposing it came into his dreams tonight?

He couldn't take the risk.

'Mummy! Daddy!' he called.

Button told them all about his scary tree-bear worry.

Daddy said, 'Shall I give you
something nice to think about
before you go to sleep?
Nice thoughts always keep
the bad ones away.'

'Yes please,' Button nodded,
feeling much braver about
the scary tree-bear already.

'Well,' wondered Daddy, 'shall I tell you about
a day when there were no scary things?
A day *so* happy that if you think of it tonight
only sweet dreams will come.'

'What day was that, Daddy?' asked Button.
Daddy kissed the top of his nose and said,
'The day you were born . . .'

'It was one of those days that started misty, but I knew
a hot and sunny day was just around the corner.'

'A bit like today?' asked Button.
'When I woke up I couldn't even
see over the berry bush!'

'Yes, just like today,' Daddy smiled, 'and on the day you were born, I gathered the juiciest berries and stickiest honey.'

'A bit like today?' asked Button,
as he remembered lying in the
warm sun eating his sweet
breakfast berries.

'Yes,' said Daddy, 'but even more delicious.'

'On the day you were born,'
Daddy continued, 'your big sisters were so
happy they found special presents for you . . .'

'Like my lucky pine-cone,' said Button,
'and my little log-boat! And did they want
to play with me too?'

'Oh yes!' laughed Daddy. 'They wanted to play with you right there and then, but Mummy said you needed to grow a little first . . .'

'And now I've grown!' said
Button. 'We played so much
today we had to jump in
Two Rivers Pool to cool down.'

'When evening came,' remembered Daddy,
'I took you in my arms to watch your
first-ever sunset and sing you a lullaby.'

'Just like *every* evening,' yawned Button.
He loved watching the sun go down with Daddy
and singing songs that made them laugh.

'And on your very first night,' said Daddy quietly,
'you were so tired you fell fast asleep. Mummy and
I watched over you, and no scary tree-bear and
bad dreams came to disturb our little one.'

'Just like tonight?' said Button.
'Yes,' whispered Daddy.

And Daddy was right . . .
only sweet dreams came.

Ten Top Tips

If your toddler has anxieties at bedtime, like Button in this story,
here are some hints and tips.

1 Keep to a consistent time for going to bed and waking your toddler in the morning.

2 Make sure your child's bedtime routine is calm and soothing.

3 Turn off all screens for an hour before bedtime.

4 Avoid content (cartoons or books, for example) that is scary just before bedtime.

5 Try some relaxation techniques with your child before bedtime and remember that baths are great for relaxation.

6 Avoid sugary foods or drinks at bedtime. Milky drinks are best to calm little tummies.

7 Share a story with your child once they are tucked up in bed.

8 Give reassuring hugs and kisses and let your child know it's time to go to sleep when you say good night.

9 A dim night light can help some children get to sleep.

10 If your toddler's sleep is disturbed by a bad dream, help them understand that the dream is not real and reassure them that they are safe.